One Dad,
Two Dads,
Brown Dad,
Blue Dads

By Johnny Valentine
Illustrated by Melody Sarecky

To Jacob,
who has only one mom and one dad.
But don't feel sorry for him.
They're both great parents.

TEXT © 1994 BY JOHNNY VALENTINE.
ILLUSTRATIONS © 1994 BY MELODY SARECKY.
ALL RIGHTS RESERVED.

MANUFACTURED IN CHINA.

THIS PAPERBACK BOOK IS PUBLISHED BY ALYSON WONDERLAND,
AN IMPRINT OF ALYSON PUBLICATIONS,
P.O. BOX 4371, LOS ANGELES, CALIFORNIA 90078-4371.
DISTRIBUTION IN THE UNITED KINGDOM BY TURNAROUND PUBLISHER SERVICES LTD.,
UNIT 3, OLYMPIA TRADING ESTATE, COBURG ROAD, WOOD GREEN,
LONDON N22 6TZ ENGLAND.

FIRST EDITION (HARDCOVER): JULY 1994
FIRST PAPERBACK EDITION: MAY 2004

04 05 06 07 08 ❖ 10 9 8 7 6 5 4 3 2 1

ISBN 1-55583-848-0
(HARDCOVER EDITION PUBLISHED WITH ISBN 1-55583-253-9.)

One dad,

two dads.

Brown dad,

blue dads.

"Blue dads?
BLUE dads!?
I don't know who
has dads that are blue!"

"I do!
My name is Lou.
I have two dads
who both are blue.

They both have blue hair,
that's the color it grows.

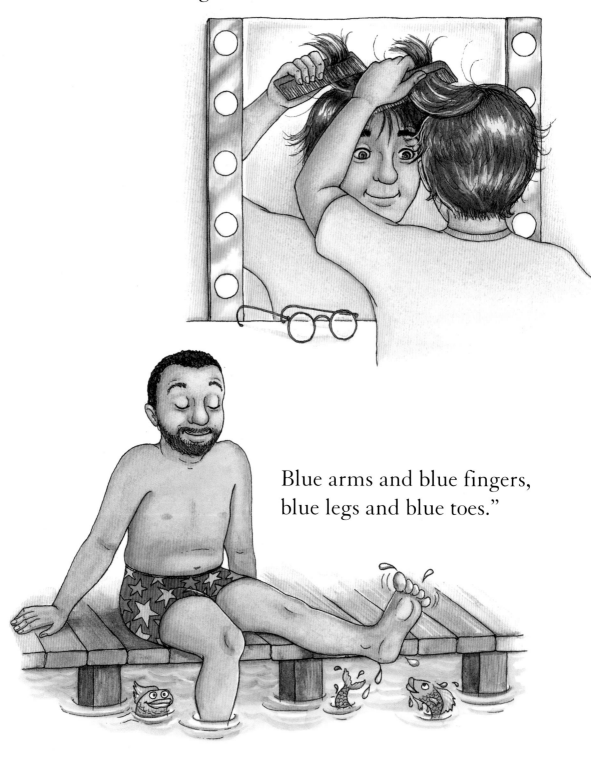

Blue arms and blue fingers,
blue legs and blue toes."

"What is it like to have blue dads?" I said.
"Do they talk? Do they sing?

And eat cookies in bed?

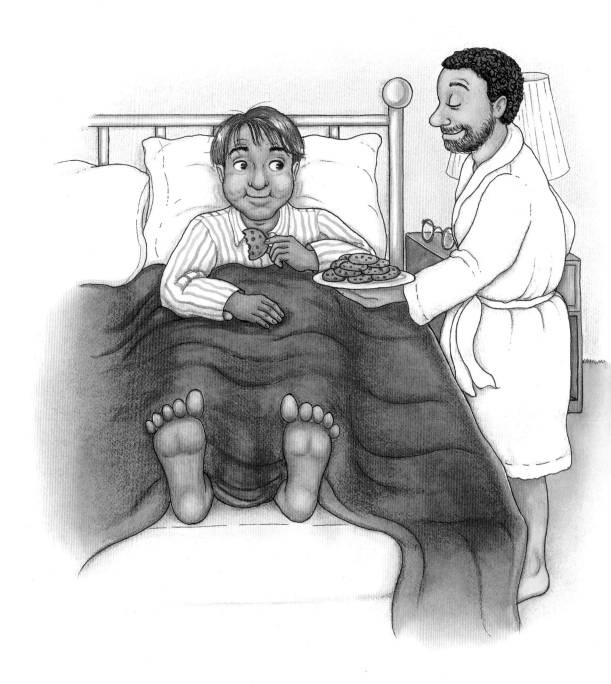

Do they work?

Do they play?

Do they cook?

Do they cough?

If they hug you too hard,
does the color rub off?"

"Of course blue dads work!
And they play and they laugh.
They do all of those things," said Lou.
"Did you think that they simply
would stop being dads,
just because they are blue?"

"My dad can stand on his head," I told Lou.
"My dad plays me songs on his purple kazoo.
He even knows how to make chocolate fondue!
Can blue dads do all those things, too?"

"What funny ideas you have," replied Lou.
"Do you think dads are different,
because they are blue?
My dads both play piano,
and one of them cooks.
(He makes wonderful chocolate cream pies.)

I have never seen either one stand on his head.
But I'm sure they both could
 ...if the need should arise."

"What I'd like to know now,"
I went on to say,
"is, just how did your dads
end up looking this way?

Did they go through the wash
with a ballpoint pen?
Or were they both blue
since the young age of ten?

Did they drink too much
blueberry juice as young boys?
Or as kids, did they play
with too many blue toys?"

"Just where did you get
all these questions?!" Lou said.
"How did *such* explanations
pop into your head?
They were blue when I got them
and blue they are still.
And it's not from a juice,
or a toy, or a pill.

They are blue because—well—
because they are blue.
And I think they're
remarkable fathers—don't you?

Yes, my dads both are blue,
and although you may try,
it is hard to see blue dads
against a blue sky.

But except for that problem,
our life is routine,
and they're just like all other dads—
black, white, or green."

"Green dads? GREEN dads!?
That I never have seen.
No, I never have seen
a dad who was green!"

"I have!
My name is Jean.
My dad's not blue.
My dad is green.

I'd love to let you take a look.
But we've run out of room now, in this little book."